Disney Descendants The Rise of Red

The Novelisation

Disney

DESCENDANTS: THE RISE OF RED

The Novelisation

Adapted by Kelsey Rodkey

Based on *Descendants: The Rise of Red*,

by Dan Frey and Russell Sommer

SCHOLASTIC

SYDNEY AUCKLAND NEW YORK TORONTO LONDON MEXICO CITY

NEW DELHI HONG KONG BUENOS AIRES PUERTO RICO

Published by Scholastic Australia in 2024.

Scholastic Australia Pty Limited
PO Box 579 Gosford NSW 2250
ABN 11 000 614 577
www.scholastic.com.au

Part of the Scholastic Group
Sydney • Auckland • New York • Toronto • London • Mexico City
New Delhi • Hong Kong • Buenos Aires • Puerto Rico

Designed by Phil Buchanan.

NATIONAL LIBRARY OF AUSTRALIA

A catalogue record for this book is available from the National Library of Australia

ISBN 978-1-76152-430-1

MIX
Paper | Supporting responsible forestry
FSC® C001695
FSC www.fsc.org

Printed and bound in Australia by the Opus Group

This product is made of material from well-managed FSC®-certified forests, recycled materials, and other controlled sources.

To Bridget and Ella,

for showing us that we make our own destiny

Chapter One

RED: Welcome back to Auradon! You know the drill: I'm Mal—psych! I'm most definitely *not* Mal, queen of Auradon. In fact, she's not even around right now. She and King Ben are off with Jay and Evie, searching for new kingdoms to make alliances with, so you're stuck with me, Red. Deal with it.

I'm the Queen of Hearts' daughter, but don't hold it against me. Growing up in Wonderland, the one country still completely cut off from Auradon, has made for an interesting childhood, to say the least. Prior to now, I've mostly been . . . homeschooled.

Yes, we'll call it homeschooling. The curriculum consists of lessons taught by my mother about how to be bad and how to rule with an iron spade so I can become the next Queen of Hearts on the throne. Nothing else really matters to her. I don't know why she is the way she is—but I know I don't want to be just like her.

I've never known anything but Wonderland—until now, at least. But this year, I'm going away to school. In *Auradon*.

I'm excited to bring my own special brand of bad to that palace full of goody-goodies. If it's in the cards, that is . . .

Chapter Two

RED: I never would have thought I'd end up at Auradon Prep, but now that a true baddie is in charge, maybe things will change for the ~~better~~ worse. Pirates know how to throw a party, right?

Over Auradon Prep the sun rose high into the sky, promising a new day of academic excellence. Outside the principal's office, groundskeepers got the campus ready for a new school year. And inside the principal's office . . .

Boom!

The office door was kicked open by Uma, now in her early twenties and a little wiser, but just as fiery as ever. The pirate captain looked around the room, sizing it up, and spoke.

"I've been sent to the principal's office before"—she smirked—"but never like this."

"I made us tea," Fairy Godmother said, welcoming Uma in. "Sit, please."

Uma flopped onto Fairy Godmother's gilded sofa, propping her boots up on the cushions.

"It's not an easy job, Uma. But I hope you find it fulfilling," Fairy Godmother said.

"I've run a crew of cutthroats since I was sixteen. I think I can handle a few prep school kids," Uma said.

She called out to her pirates in the hallway. They entered the room and immediately started redecorating. First they hung a massive black Jolly Roger flag on the wall, and then they replaced the bookends on Fairy Godmother's bookshelves with skulls. Fairy Godmother winced.

"You just enjoy retirement," Uma said to her.

"I'm not *retiring*," Fairy Godmother said. "I have been *chosen* as the new president of Auradon University."

She handed Uma some paperwork, which Uma set aside immediately.

"And to ensure a seamless transition, I've prepared a list, color-coded by priority." Fairy Godmother presented the parchment to Uma with a flourish.

"My first order of business will be making sure kids from all the kingdoms are welcome to attend AP," Uma said.

"That's already our school policy."

"I said *all*. Even . . . Wonderland," Uma said.

Fairy Godmother's jaw dropped.

"Wonderland?" She chuckled nervously. "No. Oh, no. Wonderland is hostile."

"I've heard," Uma said dismissively. "Their queen's a tyrant."

"The Queen of Hearts refused to join Auradon when we united. She raised an army and we had to wall off the Rabbit-Hole! If only Queen Mal and King Ben were here . . ." Fairy Godmother trailed off.

"Too bad they're not. And why do you think Mal put me in charge if she didn't want to shake things up around here?" Uma asked.

The pirates finished hanging up framed images of Uma's friends—Mal, Ben, Jay, and Carlos, among others.

"No offense, Fairy G, but you don't know Mal and Ben like I do," Uma said. "I used to hate Mal—I'm sure you've heard. But you know what happened? We reconciled. We saw the goodness in each other. When she and Ben finally opened up the Isle, they gave *all* villains a second chance. It's time that Wonderland got one, too."

Uma placed a handwritten letter sealed with wax into Fairy Godmother's hands. "This is for Princess Red."

"Are you sure?" Fairy Godmother asked, looking meaningfully at Uma.

Uma's eyes landed on a photo of Carlos, and

a look of resolve settled on her face. She knew her decision was the right one.

"It's what Carlos would have wanted. So don't do it for me. Do it in honor of him," Uma said.

Fairy Godmother nodded somberly and then waved her wand.

"Bibbidi . . . bobbidi . . . boo!" she said. Sparks flew from the end of her wand, and the invitation magically folded up like a paper airplane and soared out the window.

Chapter Three

RED: You've seen Auradon, and you've seen the Isle of the Lost, but you've never seen my messed-up hometown: Wonderland.

Past the golden-domed Sultan's palace in Agrabah, past the dense Sherwood Forest, and even farther past the spires of Cinderellasburg and the ivy-clad walls of Auradon Prep grew a massive tree with a burrow at the base of the trunk. The burrow was closed off by a metal gate overgrown with vines. Through that gate was a portal of color and light called the Rabbit-Hole, which led to . . . Wonderland.

Wonderland shone in the moonlight. At the center of the city loomed an imposing palace, with neat and tidy streets surrounding it.

The citizens of Wonderland, all clad in the same red-and-black uniforms, hurried through the city in orderly lines, rushing home from work. One by one, they closed and locked their doors, scared to disobey the curfew. Above their heads, the heart-shaped lanterns of the streetlights turned on, casting an ominous red glow over the empty streets. A lone figure snuck through the shadows, her spiky-studded hood pulled over her head. She darted under a lamp, carefully tucking a lock of her fiery red hair out of sight. Red, a sixteen-year-old renegade with brooding eyes and crimson lipstick, kept her face hidden in shadow as she peered around the corner.

Numerous heart-shaped topiaries and urns of red roses littered the empty city center, and Red used her stealth to her advantage as she grabbed a pair of gardening shears and ran down a row of primly manicured hedges, lopping off the bloom of every rose with a sharp snip.

She turned a corner to stand beneath a three-story portrait of the Queen of Hearts that hung over the side of a building. Looking up through the lacy red eye mask she wore, Red held up a bulging water balloon filled with red paint. She hurled it at the portrait of the Queen and watched with satisfaction as the paint exploded and dripped down her stern visage.

Moving on to the tall vases full of roses, Red wound up a croquet mallet and smashed the first one with an expert baseball swing. *Yes.* She raised the mallet high and crushed a second. *Yes.* She knelt into a graceful spin and took out a third. *Yes!* The triple-swing combo of destruction left her out of breath and giddy. But she couldn't linger too long; the city guard was sure to be on their way.

Just as Red ran out of the square, soldiers of the Crimson Army, wearing military uniforms emblazoned with the symbols of playing cards, were led into the plaza by the Jack of Diamonds. They searched the area for the criminal who was causing all the mayhem. Red slinked behind pillars, doing her best to avoid them. Then she made her move, tossing a ground-spinner firework into the middle of their formation. It sparked wildly, scattering the soldiers as it exploded and allowing Red to slip away unseen.

The Jack, a clean-shaven man with long blond hair, looked around the area, furious, until he spotted Red on the roof of a nearby building. He pursued her to the top and charged, clearing the gap and following her across the rooftops of Wonderland with his soldiers right behind him. He was not giving up on catching Red.

With her back to the edge of a rooftop, Red was cornered by the Jack and soldiers, but—*There.* A three-story drop to the ground that she could survive, with a little help from the Queen's tacky portrait. A gleam filled Red's eyes as inspiration struck, and she clutched her trusty gardening shears.

Red flipped backward off the edge of the building, swung wide, and jabbed the point of her shears into the portrait. Slicing the portrait down the Queen's face, Red slowed her descent until she landed safely, leaving the soldiers gaping at her from the roof.

She raced off, fleeing the scene.

The Jack of Diamonds continued his pursuit, ordering his men back to ground level, where they headed in different directions. He reached an overlook and peered across the city, not knowing that Red hid below, pressed against the wall in the shadows. He couldn't tell the Queen of Hearts that he'd let the vandal escape. He knew that it was either off with the vandal's head or off with *his*!

In stark contrast to the militaristic and cold palace, bedecked with flags displaying a menacing crest of a rose and thorn, Red on the run was all brightness and energy. She darted. She danced. Through alleys, she swung from balconies and launched off awnings. She was exuberant at not being caught.

Finally Red reached a dead end. She tried not to panic at this unexpected twist, but the sound of stomping boots approached. The soldiers were catching up!

Red grabbed a torch off the wall and brandished it, defiant and brave, ready to throw down. But as the soldiers approached from around the corner, a large hook out of nowhere snagged Red by her backpack and yanked her into the air. The soldiers rushed in, sure they were about to find the criminal, but found nothing. They looked around, baffled. High above them, Red dangled on the hook from a crane-like contraption. The soldiers hadn't thought to look *up* for their criminal. The contraption swung her to a parapet, where a trapdoor opened, and then the crane dropped her onto a slide at the mouth of its cavity.

Inside a workshop full of gadgets and gizmos, sparking electrical creations, and pistons venting steam, a tube lowered and spat out Red onto a sofa, bringing her face-to-face with Maddox Hatter, the son of the Mad Hatter. He pushed a button to retract the tube Red had just come from. His lavender hair and jaunty ascot gave him a playful look, but the expression on his face was all anxiety. He huffed.

"Those soldiers could've dragged you to the dungeon, Red. What on earth were you *thinking*?" he said.

"That my mom's portrait could use a little touch-up," Red said cheekily. "Hope she likes it."

"I'm seriously worried about you, Red," said

Maddox as he pulled on his embroidered coat and straightened his giant top hat. "If you continue down this path, I won't always be there to save you. You know that, right?"

"Maddox Hatter, you know you can't save me. I'm a prisoner of Wonderland. I'm a lost cause," Red said, making herself at home in Maddox's laboratory.

"You are not a lost cause." He sat down next to her. "As your tutor, I'm in charge of preparing you for your future. And as your friend, I want you to have one," Maddox said.

"What future, Mads? I literally have the most controlling mom ever. She's never gonna let me leave Wonderland."

"I know it hasn't been easy, growing up with a mother who is so"—Maddox thought about how to phrase the rest of his sentence—"*particular*. But you must know: she wasn't always this way."

Red gave him a skeptical look.

"It's true!" he said. "We're all products of our past. And your mother's was certainly unfortunate."

"She just wants to turn me into the next evil queen, like her. And I don't want to be queen. I just want to be in charge of my own life. But what I want doesn't matter to her."

"Oh, Red." Maddox softened at her admission and debated what to say next. "I wasn't going to show you this until you were a little older . . ." He trailed off. "But I finished it." He stood, and Red, curious, followed him.

He led her to a corner of the room, where a lab table stood covered in tools, gears, and bits and pieces. An item on a small pedestal was draped with a crimson velvet cloth. Red was intrigued when Maddox dramatically whipped off the cloth to reveal a golden pocketwatch attached to a hefty chain.

"My time machine," he said proudly. "It takes you to the moment in time that can give you what your heart wants most."

Surprise flashed on Red's face.

"If you really want a different life, Red, I want you to have that choice. But I should warn you: when you alter the fabric of time, there can be some unpredictable consequences," Maddox said.

Red considered this seriously . . . then reached for the device.

"I think I can live with that," she said lightly.

Maddox got to the pocketwatch first, clamping his hand down over it.

"*Everything* could change. You could lose your mother entirely," he said. His expression practically begged her to understand how important this was.

Red paused, considering his words again. In her silence, Maddox slipped the time machine into his jacket pocket and turned away.

"It's too dangerous. When you're more mature," he said. "I know you're frustrated, Red, but I'm trying to look out for you. I care about you very much."

Despite her resistance, Red was moved by his warmth. She went in for a hug and held him tight.

"Thanks, Mads," she said. "At least someone still does."

They pulled away from each other, a tender moment ending. And as they did, they heard the sound of footsteps approaching. Soldiers.

"If the Queen finds out I'm harboring a fugitive, I'll be in serious trouble. You'd better get out of here, Red," he said.

"I dare you to make me," Red said.

"As you wish . . . *Princess*!" he said, pressing a button on his sleeve.

"What'd I say about calling me princeeee—"

A tube descended into the room and vacuumed her right into the ceiling, her flaming red hair first. One of Maddox's many contraptions whirred, producing a steaming hot cup of tea. Maddox sipped it slowly, enjoying his newfound peace.

At the palace, in Red's room, she thumped down onto her heart-shaped bed from the tube. Exhausted, she flopped back onto the red and black pillows that covered the mattress. She eased her hand into her pocket and pulled out . . . the pocketwatch.

She was impressed with herself for picking Maddox's pocket. Grinning mischievously, she pondered the wildly spinning hands of the clock and listened to the *tick, tick, tick*.

Her finger moved to the button on top as she contemplated the chance to change her life . . . but she hesitated. Red wasn't sure she was ready to let go of her mom forever, no matter how bad she was. Red's courage, once so lively and loud, faltered with Maddox's warnings echoing in her mind. *Not today.*

Chapter Four

CHLOE: Some kids argue with their parents. Others turn theirs into lizards. But me? I like to sword fight with mine. What can I say? It's family bonding!

Chloe Charming squinted from the bright Cinderellasburg sun as her sword reflected it. The sixteen-year-old daughter of Cinderella was skilled with her weapon, but her masked opponent was, too. He brandished a fencing sword at her, but she parried and countered with masterful slices, her curly blue hair swaying with the motions. In her quilted blue vest and sporty pleated skirt, Chloe felt every inch the tourney champion she knew she could be.

Her opponent deflected each jab, circling around her. Chloe attacked with her own barrage of swings and retreated backward up the castle steps. One might have assumed Chloe was trapped, but she leapt off the railing to safety on a nearby castle wall . . . and then made space for her opponent to join her.

They resumed their fight on the narrow ledge, their blades flashing in the sun, until Chloe threw a combination of practiced attacks at her opponent—and led the fight back down to the ground.

Chloe grinned, pulling off her mask and taking in her opponent.

"Gotcha," she said.

Out of nowhere, her opponent lunged at her, pulling out another weapon—a *breadstick.*

"Bet you didn't see *that* coming," he said.

Chloe frowned at her father, King Charming, as he removed his mask.

"Dad. That's cheating!" Chloe said.

With a goofy grin, he took a bite from his makeshift weapon. "No. That's delicious," he said. When Chloe rolled her eyes, he continued. "Don't be so serious, Chloe! We signed you up for swords and shields because it was supposed to be *fun*."

"Well, yeah, it is. But when I'm out there, I'm not just another competitor. I represent Cinderellasburg."

"You sound like your mother," he said.

"Don't listen to him," said Cinderella, clad in a sparkling blue dress and elegant sheer gloves, as she appeared from the grand front entrance. She smiled at her husband, showing him that she was playfully disagreeing, and continued, "Your father's never cared about what other people think."

"I don't have to. I'm charming," he said.

"That's debatable," Cinderella said.

Sidling up to her, King Charming extended his arm to Cinderella and pressed a kiss to the back of her hand. They waltzed while Chloe rolled her eyes, begging them to stop.

"Dad," Chloe whined. "Mom!"

They continued dancing, ignoring her protests as they hummed a familiar tune.

"Can you not?" Chloe said.

"You know, this is the first song your mom and I ever danced to, back when we were in school," King Charming said.

"We fell in love at Castlecoming," Cinderella chimed in.

"Yeah, I know. You tell me every time. And I know you guys have a healthy relationship and all, but come *on*," Chloe said.

"It's a good thing, too, or we wouldn't have been able to create this amazing family," Cinderella said, thinking not only of her wonderful husband and daughter, but of her son, Chad. "I know you packed last night, but do you think you might have room for one more pair of shoes?"

Cinderella produced a large box, opening it with a flourish in front of Chloe.

As the box's contents were revealed, Chloe squealed with uncontained joy. It was a pair of glass boots!

"Mom! They're just like yours—but even *cooler*!" Chloe said.

"You earned them. You got straight A's last year—"

"And volunteered at the Auradon Historical Society," added King Charming.

"But the thing I'm most proud of is that you're such a good person," Cinderella continued.

Chloe beamed. Her mother's pride meant a great deal to her.

"That's why you're a great princess," Cinderella said, "and why you'll make a great queen."

"These are big shoes to fill," Chloe said with a grin.

Cinderella smiled softly and then nodded at the boots. "You gonna try 'em on or what?" she asked.

Chloe did, eagerly.

Chapter Five

RED: You know, you go your whole life waiting for something exciting to happen, but when your mom decides to be full of surprises one day, its . . . alarming. It's like, who even are you?

"Her Royal Highness, Her Grace, Her Excellency, Her Magnanimous Majesty, Empress of Wonderland, the Queen of Hearts!" a guard cried as the Queen was carried into the square on a heart-shaped chair festooned with roses.

She surveyed the scene of the previous night's crime. Her face was frozen in the same severe expression she wore in the now-slashed portrait, its canvas hanging in two halves.

That day she had chosen a menacing royal wardrobe, red with black accents, and a deadly-sharp ruby-studded crown. On one hand, a glittery glove ended in spiky, sparkling tips.

Before her, the Jack of Diamonds knelt among the rubble of shattered statues and clipped roses.

"Who is responsible?" she asked him.

"We don't know, Your Royal Highness. I've doubled the guard, tripled the patrols, and personally offered ten diamonds for any information that leads to the capture of the criminal," he said.

"Her Royal Highness Princess Red!" the crier interrupted as Red was escorted in by two guards.

She was rocking her combat boots and her red leather jacket—the one with the broken heart emblazoned on the back—over a red-and-black mesh top. Her fingerless black gloves were studded with razor-sharp rubies.

"I see you couldn't be *bothered* to dress for court. I find that outfit offensive," the Queen said.

"I wish being me didn't offend you," Red said.

The Queen of Hearts huffed. "Sorry to rouse you out of bed before noon, but while you were sleeping, the Royal Plaza was *vandalized*," she said to Red, shooting a look at Jack. "And *this* sorry excuse for a soldier failed to protect my portrait. So the question is . . . what do we do? Poke thorns in his eyes? Off with his head?" Idly, she shuffled through a deck of cards in one gloved hand. "Since you'll be queen one day, I'll let you decide."

Red looked down with dread at the still-kneeling Jack of Diamonds. She didn't want to dole out punishments like her mother; she found no joy in others' pain. But if she didn't do *something*, her mother would sentence the Jack to worse.

"It's up to me?" she asked. Her mother nodded. "Okay. Well, in that case . . . *off with his* . . . hat," Red said.

She plucked off the Jack's cap and placed it on her own head, smirking.

"You are such a disappointment," the Queen said, shaking her head.

Red flinched, the words worse than a slap. The Queen picked up a clipped rose bloom and considered it before launching into one of her unwanted lessons.

"I was the same way at your age. I desperately wanted to be a queen that everyone would adore." The Queen touched the flower's petals. "But if I've learned anything, it's this: it is better to be feared than loved."

The Queen pressed her fingertip to a sharp thorn. Instead of pain, admiration flashed on her face.

"Love ain't it. Now, try again." She challenged Red with a look.

Fear shone in Red's eyes as she turned to face the Jack once more. She took a deep breath and tried to adopt her mother's harsh tone.

"For your crime, you are sentenced to . . ." She trailed off.

"Get it right, or I'll show you punishment!" her mother cried, losing any patience she'd pretended to have.

Before Red could respond, Maddox charged into the plaza.

"Your Majesty! Apologies! Apologies for interrupting court."

He removed his hat and sank into a bow. "Your Majesty. Royal delivery!" he said.

The enchanted envelope from Auradon flew from his outstretched hand. It hovered in front of the Queen—and then the magic invitation began speaking in Uma's voice.

"Dear Queen of Hearts, Empress of Wonderland: As the new principal of Auradon Prep, it is my honor to invite your daughter, Red, the princess of Wonderland, to attend our school. We hope you will join us for the Welcome Day Ceremony," it said. "Upon acceptance, this invitation shall serve as your key."

"From pirate to principal? Hm. Another villain has gone *soft*," the Queen said.

Maddox slunk up to Red as the Queen considered the invitation.

"Maybe you have a future after all," he said quietly. "If you go to Auradon Prep, you'll get to leave Wonderland."

Slowly, Red lit up with excitement. She tamped it down, remembering who her mother was.

"Doesn't matter," Red said to Maddox. "The only thing she hates more than Auradon is the idea of me having my own life, so . . . I'm pretty sure that's gonna be a no."

The Queen whirled around to face Red, an unnerving smile on her face.

"We accept!" she announced to the court at large.

Red could not believe what she was hearing.

"Wait, hold on. Really?" she asked.

A check mark magically appeared in the YES box on the invitation, and the letter floated away. "But you've always said Auradon is the worst," Red pointed out.

"Well, with my daughter there, it might not always be," the Queen said.

"You're gonna let me go. *You?*"

"Pack your bags." She took her seat on the throne once more and was carried slowly out of the square.

Astonished, Red glanced at Maddox. "Am I hallucinating? Or did my mom just grow a heart?" she said to him.

"And put on something respectable, for *once*.

Don't embarrass me," the Queen called out as she disappeared from sight.

Red slumped, dejected. She had spoken too soon.

"Okay . . . half a heart," she said to Maddox.

In Cinderellasburg, Chloe bounded down to the carriage in her new boots. She'd swapped her tourney outfit for a quilted blue jacket and a pair of two-tone pants, and the teal look she was sporting was the perfect complement to her dazzling silver shoes.

"They fit *perfectly*!" she said. "I love them!"

Her dad, standing outside the carriage, smiled at her infectious joy. "There's my girl," he said, helping her through the open door.

"So beautiful," her mom murmured. Cinderella turned to her husband.

"You sure you can't come? We could visit Chad at college another time," she said.

"He really wants me to come see him play tourney, so . . ." King Charming shrugged. He turned to Chloe.

"Take care of your mom for me," he said.

Chloe nodded, and Cinderella got into the carriage with her. They were off to Auradon Prep!

Outside the city walls in Wonderland, the Queen of Hearts' vehicle crunched over the landscape. She and Red trundled along in the bright red jalopy, heading for a wild-looking forest.

The silence between mother and daughter dragged on. They weren't the type of family that had even casual conversations, so what Red *wanted* to say—that as she was leaving Wonderland, she needed to know her mom loved her and cared for her—was too heavy to broach during the drive. Instead, Red focused on the road ahead of them. She gaped when she saw the vine-covered tree they were quickly approaching.

"So how do we get into the Rabbit-Hole?" asked Red. "It's still locked."

They were getting closer and closer to the barred entrance, but instead of slowing down, the Queen sped up.

"Mom, what are you doing?" Red cried.

"Oh, you have so much to learn," the Queen said, cackling.

She barreled straight toward the gate with the vehicle. Red tensed, but as they drove, her invitation to Auradon Prep soared in front of them and transformed into a key. It slid smoothly into the lock, and the gate swung open.

"Finally," the Queen muttered. The car shrank just in the nick of time, entering the tunnel with no issues. Red looked around at the tunnel in awe. She had never thought she would be there—on her way *out* of Wonderland.

Finally, the car emerged from the Rabbit-Hole, and Auradon border guards waved at them to stop. Red could hardly believe what had just happened. They were in *Auradon*. She looked at her mother but found only her usual disapproving face.

"Oh, Red. I thought I told you to put on something respectable," the Queen said. Red deflated and gazed out the window blankly. Would it kill her mother to show her a little love?

The Queen obliged the guards, letting them inspect the vehicle with undercarriage mirrors and look into the windows. A guard wearing aviators approached the driver's side and knocked on the window. The Queen rolled down her window and handed over her purse when the guard instructed her to. He poked around inside but found only a simple deck of playing cards. He examined them closely and then, nodding, returned them to the purse. He gave the Queen an all clear and allowed the car to proceed to the gleaming city beyond, and to Auradon Prep.

In front of the school, incoming students and parents waited patiently at a check-in table until the Queen's vehicle roared up the front steps and came to a shuddering stop. They whispered as the Queen and Red approached. Red could have sworn she heard a chorus of "off with your heads." Clearly her mother's reputation preceded her.

Cutting the line, the Queen marched up to the front of the check-in table with Red trailing her, mortified.

"You know who we are," the Queen said to the volunteers working at the table.

But before they could respond, someone spoke beside them.

"Bridget," breathed Cinderella. She stood by Chloe with a shocked expression on her face. "I didn't expect to see you here."

Red was astounded by this interaction so far. *No one* called her mother by her first name. Red hid her surprise quickly.

"*Ella.* It's 'Your Royal Highness' now," the Queen said.

"Of course. You must be very proud," Cinderella said. The two stood there, with some kind of unspoken conversation happening between them.

Chloe waved awkwardly at Red and introduced herself. "Uh . . . hi! I'm Chloe Charming. You must be Princess Red of Wonderland? I've always *wondered* what it's like over there," she joked.

"You should come sometime. I'll introduce you to the Jabberwocky," Red said.

"Fun! What's a Jabberwocky?" Chloe asked.

"A monster that eats annoying girls."

Chloe's face fell when she realized Red was mocking her. Before she could think of a comeback, the Queen summoned Red with a snap of her fingers.

The Queen turned away and Red raced to keep

up, her interest piqued. She asked her mom about the tension between the two women, because it was clear from that exchange that they had some kind of history. The Queen of Hearts explained that they had once been classmates at Auradon Prep, back when it had a different name. According to the Queen, Cinderella and all the other students had been two-faced, so Red needed to be on guard while she was there.

Cinderella told a different story to Chloe, though. As she and Chloe left the check-in table and headed for the Welcome Day Ceremony, she told Chloe that she shouldn't take Red's or the Queen's attitude to heart. Sometimes, she said, people lashed out in anger because of the things that had been done to them in the past—like the Queen of Hearts, who'd had an awful prank played on her during their time at school. Cinderella wouldn't elaborate any further, choosing to stay positive and talk of Chloe's future at Auradon Prep instead.

Chloe reluctantly accepted the change of conversation, but it didn't escape her notice that Cinderella had tried to hide a guilty expression from her.

Chapter Six

RED: I know Auradon's thing is inviting the villains and their kids because second chances and blah blah, but I really don't think they thought this through, inviting my mom.

The walled garden of Auradon Prep was set up for an event, laid out with tables and folding chairs for students and their families, as well as a large stage against one wall. The Queen of Hearts strutted in, her huge heart-shaped gown cutting a wide path, with Red trailing behind. Everyone in the garden turned to stare.

The refreshment table called to Red's stomach. She grabbed a brightly colored macaron and was about to take a bite when her mom abruptly snatched it away. The Queen threw it in the garbage. *Oh, right, treats are for the weak.* Red had been *so* close to eating some sugar for the first time, but she could wait until her mom left to enjoy some. She had already waited her whole life.

Her mother paraded haughtily past the other royal parents, such as Aladdin and Jasmine, and their kids—Red's new classmates. What had any of these people ever done to her? When Cinderella and Chloe entered the courtyard, the Queen made a beeline with her eyes, glaring daggers at Cinderella until she turned away.

The Queen stopped in the center of the courtyard and opened her purse. She retrieved her golden compact—the famous Looking Glass. She flipped it open to show Red the polished surface, but all Red saw was her reflection.

Suddenly, the mirror rippled with magic and showed a new image, much like a screen would. In the Looking Glass, Red saw the Auradon Throne Room. Dust hung thickly in the air, and shafts of colorful light pierced the gloom. The Queen of Hearts sat on the throne, and next to her? Next to her, in a matching ruby crown, was Red.

In the vision, she looked exactly like her mom—same hair, same elaborate style of gown, same cruel expression. Painted on Red's right cheek was a bright red heart, menacing in its sweetness. Could this really be her?

Red was floored and confused by what she saw in the mirror. Her mother offered her the Looking Glass. Red just stared.

"That's . . ." she said.

"The Looking Glass, yes. It shows *the future*—where you and I will rule together side by side."

The Queen's dream come true. But not Red's dream.

"But I don't want that . . . I don't wanna be *anything* like you," Red bravely said, pushing away the Looking Glass.

Hurt by Red's rejection, the Queen grew angry.

"You don't have a choice," she said. "We're more alike than you know."

Before their familiar argument could start up, Fairy Godmother stepped onto the stage. Everyone took their seats and waited expectantly.

"Parents and students, it has been a great privilege to serve you. But the time has come for another to take my place. So please join me in welcoming Auradon Prep's new principal," Fairy Godmother said.

She trailed off and a beat dropped, introducing Uma's band of pirates as they tumbled and flipped up to the stage. When Uma entered from the back, a hush fell over the crowd. Her pirates shouted her name: "Uma!"

"That's *Principal Uma* to you. And you'd better get it straight, or you'll be walking the plank," she said.

The students looked terrified until Fairy Godmother giggled nervously. "She's just kidding!" she promised.

"Now, I never got the chance to go to Auradon Prep," Uma said. "But as its captain, I'm proud to be charting a new course into a bright future—beyond the old ways of heroes and villains." She gave Red a knowing look. "So in that spirit, I'd like to welcome Princess Red of Wonderland."

Red smiled tentatively, but next to her, the Queen of Hearts just shuffled her deck of cards noisily, not looking at Uma. She flicked them between her outstretched hands, smiling at her own cleverness.

"Excuse me, do you mind?" Uma asked.

"I do, actually," the Queen said. She stood up, surprising the crowd.

"Mom, what are you *doing*?" Red asked, her eyes begging her mother to sit back down.

"Playing my favorite game . . ." The Queen paused for dramatic effect. *"War,"* she cried. She threw a handful of cards into the air, and they fluttered in the wind, magically forming a heart. As they tumbled to the ground, they transformed. They sprouted arms and legs, becoming the soldiers of the Crimson Army.

In terror, some of the royal families tried to flee, but the Queen of Hearts waved her hands, and giant gates, each wrought to look like cards, appeared over every exit.

Chaos reigned in the courtyard. Uma's sword was flying this way and that as she battled card guards up on the stage. Fairy Godmother rose to her feet and reached for her wand.

"Bibbidi-bobbidi—" she started.

But the Queen of Hearts turned to face her before she could finish. "No," she said, lazily waving a hand in Fairy Godmother's direction. The wand fell, and Fairy Godmother was apprehended by a guard.

When Uma was finally detained as well, the Queen of Hearts strode to the stage and looked defiantly over the crowd.

"Oh, calm down. You're acting like you've never seen a coup before!" she said.

In response, her captive audience cowered. It made her grin.

"Mom, this is crazy. Even for you," Red said.

"Crazy that it's taken this long. I have been waiting years to be invited back into Auradon. So thanks, Red. You finally did something useful," the Queen said.

Red mentally kicked herself for thinking her mom had ever been excited for *her*.

"I should've known it was never about me," Red said.

"*Everything* I do is for you," the Queen said.

"That was *my* invitation. *My* school. *My* life," Red said.

"Someday you'll thank me. We've already seen the ending. Spoiler alert: we win!" the Queen said.

Cinderella stepped forward, challenging the Queen of Hearts. "Stop it, Bridget! You're better than this!" she said.

Two guards crossed their spears in front of Cinderella, keeping her back from the Queen.

The Queen reddened with rage but waved them off. "Let her through," she said.

"This is too far! I know that what happened was hard for you, but that was ages ago," Cinderella continued.

"Feels like yesterday *to me*," the Queen said.

"It was a stupid prank!" Cinderella said.

Red, watching the argument between her mother and Cinderella, processed the words, connecting them to what her mother had said earlier.

"Stupid, I could forgive. But humiliating a girl

at her first dance . . ." The Queen's voice tremored when she said, "Turning me into a giant in front of everyone . . . that's just *cruel.*"

"You're right," Cinderella said with a shake of her head.

"But you didn't care then," the Queen continued. "You were off with your prince. Oh, but you will now."

Questions brewing in her mind, Red tried to catch her mom's eye. But her mom wouldn't look away from Cinderella.

"You will all show me the *respect* I deserve!" the Queen said, dangling her hand in front of Cinderella. "Now *kneel.*"

Cinderella gathered herself, shook her head, and locked eyes with the Queen.

"I will never kneel to a tyrant," Cinderella said.

Chloe lifted her chin, proud of her mom's strength, but the Queen of Hearts merely smiled before turning back to Red.

"She's denied a royal order. What do we do about that, darling?" the Queen asked.

Red took a breath and approached Cinderella

with dread. She knew what her mom wanted her to say.

"Look, all you have to do is swear allegiance. Is that so hard?" she asked Cinderella.

"If it means compromising everything I stand for, yes."

Red looked back to her mom, hoping for a way out of this. She felt like both she and Cinderella were being punished right then.

"Who are you loyal to, Red—these strangers or your mother?" The Queen leaned into Red. "Now make me proud. For once."

The Queen nodded toward Cinderella; she wanted Red to sentence her. Red swallowed hard, grappling with the decision before her.

"Come on, Bridget. Even your daughter knows it's wrong. She can't do it," Cinderella said.

Red bristled at the accusation. She didn't like being told what she could and couldn't do.

She slunk forward to face Cinderella, then looked back at her mother one more time before she spoke.

"Treason. She's guilty of treason," Red announced.

"Exactly right, my dear. And that means . . . *off with her head*," the Queen said.

Chloe backed away in horror as the soldiers dragged Cinderella away.

"Mom?" Chloe called as they pushed past where she stood.

"It's going to be okay, Chloe," promised Cinderella. "I love you. It's going to be okay."

"Mom!"

"Be brave, Chloe."

Red watched the scene unfolding, conflicted about what she'd done. The Queen of Hearts was delighted.

"I knew you had it in you," she said to Red.

"Let her go!" Red heard Chloe cry.

But for once, the Queen seemed proud of Red. She beamed at her daughter.

"You'll be a great queen after all," she said.

She planted a kiss on Red's cheek, leaving behind a distinctive heart-shaped mark, like in the vision from the Looking Glass. Stunned, Red turned to the audience in the courtyard. They all shrank from her gaze, afraid of her, like they had been of her mom.

In the front row, Jasmine and Aladdin whispered to each other.

"Look at her. She's *enjoying* this," Aladdin said.

"Like mother, like daughter . . ." Jasmine said.

Red shuddered, overhearing them. The last thing she wanted was to be like her mom. With serious second thoughts in her mind, Red slipped her hand into a pocket inside her jacket and freed Maddox Hatter's watch. She looked from the chaos of the coup to the magical device in her palm. Was now the time to try it out—to go back and fix what she'd done?

Outraged by her mother's sentencing, Chloe pushed forward and shouted at the Queen of Hearts. "Hey, that's not fair! Let her go!" Chloe said.

"Oh, bless your heart," the Queen said with amused condescension.

Infuriated, Chloe drew her sword, but Red instinctively intercepted her. "Wait!" she cried. She struggled to keep the weapon locked in the sheath at Chloe's side.

Chloe tried to break free, but Red held on tight, saving Chloe from her own bravado. Red knew that her mom wouldn't be lenient with Chloe. In their tussle, Chloe grabbed Red's hand . . . and caused Red's thumb to accidentally press down on the knob of the pocketwatch.

An ominous *ticktock* filled the courtyard.

Golden spirals erupted from the watch, like a globe of pure spinning energy. The girls froze mid-fight, as though time had stopped. Whirling gears of light turned faster and faster around them. *Click!*

The energy was sucked back in, and the watch vanished, taking the girls with it.

Chapter Seven

CHLOE: The last thing I wanted today was to be *back in time* with the Queen of Hearts' daughter! What did I do to deserve this? I need to get back to my mother!

Red and Chloe emerged from a swirling golden light, still grappling with each other.

"Let go of me!" Chloe said, wrenching free from Red's grasp.

Both girls stumbled and, as they righted themselves, looked at the empty courtyard around them.

The Queen and soldiers, the other families . . . all gone.

"Um . . ." Chloe started. "What just happened? Where'd everybody go?"

"Whoa. *It works,*" Red said, looking at the pocket-watch in her hands.

"What works? Where *are* we?" Chloe asked.

"Not where. *When,*" Red said.

Chloe squinted in puzzlement. She must have misunderstood Red.

A voice from across the courtyard drew their attention to a young Fairy Godmother sitting on a bench under a tree. At least, she looked a bit like Fairy Godmother . . .

"Bibbidi . . . bobbidi . . ." Fay said, far less confident in her words than the older version of her had been moments earlier . . . in the future. "Boo!"

Magic shot out of her wand and hit the schoolbook in Fay's lap. The book flew away from her and bounced farther into the courtyard.

"No!" Fay said. "I wanted to speed-read, not for my reading to speed off!"

She grabbed her runaway book, stopping in front

of Red and Chloe when she noticed them standing there.

"Hi! Excuse me!" Chloe said. "Um . . . where'd everybody go?"

"Every . . . who?" Fay asked.

"All the royal families of Auradon. They were just here."

"What's Auradon?" Fay asked. But before Chloe could respond—though how did you answer a question like *that*?—Fay's book leapt out of her arms once more. "I gotta go catch my homework."

She hurried away, leaving Chloe, deeply confused, to turn to Red.

"Everyone's heard of Auradon. And the only person who says 'Bibbidi-bobbidi-boo' is Fairy Godmother . . ." Chloe said.

"Maybe she's not a godmother yet?" Red wondered.

"What do you mean?"

"Look around you. Fairy Godmother sucks at magic. Auradon doesn't exist. Which means . . ." Red waited for Chloe to catch on, but she didn't. "Really? I thought you were smart. *We're back in time.*"

Chloe shook her head, looking around. "No. Wait. *No.* How?" she asked.

Red showed her the pocketwatch. "*This* . . . is a time machine."

Chloe couldn't believe that. "You're joking, right?" she asked.

"Does it look like I'm joking?" Red asked, pointing to her deadpan face.

Chloe eyed the watch. "Why would you take us back in time?"

"I didn't take you. You just grabby-grabbed your way in. And this is not what I had in mind." When Chloe just stood there with a questioning look on her face, Red continued, "I just wanted to stop my mom."

"What about my mom?" Chloe's question exploded out. "You sentenced her to death!"

"Maybe not my finest moment," admitted Red. "But I'm going to fix it."

"How?"

"I thought the watch would take me back a couple minutes so I could steal my mom's deck of cards"—Red glanced around again—"not a couple of decades."

"Well, we need to go back and save my mom," said Chloe.

"No," said Red. "The watch sent us to this time for a reason."

"Give me that!" Chloe said, making a grab for the pocketwatch.

Red pulled it away with a disbelieving look. "I don't need the help of some princess Goody Two-shoes. I'll handle this myself," she said, taunting Chloe.

Chloe tried to grab the pocketwatch again, and Red tried to evade the attack. But this time, Chloe managed to snag the chain of the watch.

Now in close quarters, the girls tugged back and forth. Finally, Red yanked the watch free and fled. Chloe chased her through the courtyard, jumping over tables and sliding under benches. "Give me that watch!"

"You're out of your league, Princess!"

Once Chloe had Red cornered between a column and the courtyard wall, she drew her sword. She pointed it dramatically at Red's chest in a check-mate move, but Red remained defiant and unfazed.

"What are you gonna do now—run me through and steal my watch? I think there's a word for that, actually . . . starts with a *v* . . . Oh, right—villain," Red said.

Ignoring Red's words, Chloe abruptly lunged and skewered the loop of the pocketwatch with the tip of her sword. Her father would have been so proud of the expert move. Chloe plucked the watch from Red and slung it into her palm.

Red chased after Chloe and spun her around, and they went head-to-head. Red ran up a wall, kicking off the bricks to pluck a hanging flag from its base to use as a weapon. She landed and attacked Chloe, forcing her up some stairs as they fought. Red whirled after her and caught the watch with the tip of the flag, sending it soaring from Chloe's hand. The girls watched it fly across the courtyard . . . and hook onto a statue, mounted high up on the courtyard wall.

They cautiously lowered their weapons, frustrated with the fight. They tried to duke it out in a new way—with words—but soon realized something. They both wanted the same thing: to get back to their own time period. To stop the Queen of Hearts from sentencing Cinderella to death. To be reunited with their own mothers—for better or for worse. And they could only do that together, with Red's innovative thinking and Chloe's practiced skills. They needed to work as a team, whether they liked each other or not.

With Red close on her heels, Chloe launched herself over a balcony, and they raced back across the courtyard toward the watch. It was too high for them to reach, but Chloe was determined. Red watched her swing her sword at the statue until she managed to make contact with the watch's chain and fling it free once more.

Satisfied now that she had the watch back in her hand, Chloe looked at Red seriously.

"So you really want to stop your mom?" she asked.

"Yeah. I do," Red said.

"Why? If she takes over, you'll be the next princess of Auradon."

"And if I'm the next princess of Auradon, it's only a matter of time before she turns me into her mini-me. I am not gonna let that happen."

Chloe gave her a hard look. "Okay. I accept your mission." She strode away.

The girls exited the courtyard and made their way to the front of the school, which was buzzing with students heading to class. Chloe smiled politely at people as they walked—until Red put a stop to that. Then Chloe spotted the sign right next to the school gates: MERLIN ACADEMY.

Red stared in confusion, but realization dawned on Chloe. "Oh, of course—Merlin Academy! That's what Auradon Prep used to be called, back before the Beast united all the kingdoms and made Auradon—"

Red interrupted her rambling. "How do you know all this?"

"I love history! Don't you?" Chloe asked.

Red's expression said it all. History had never been her thing.

They continued into the school, wandered through the dorm building, and took it all in. Neither of them had gotten a proper tour of Auradon Prep before the Queen of Hearts ruined their chance.

When they made it to the student lounge, both girls gaped. The room was beautiful, with high vaulted ceilings and elaborate wall hangings. Luxurious armchairs and massive tables dotted the space, filled with students chatting and studying. Some were even practicing their magic; sparks flew from magic wands in a corner of the lounge.

"No *way*!" Chloe said.

She was looking at a poster announcing Castlecoming.

"Castlecoming—it's like the biggest event of the year!" Chloe said excitedly.

"Sorry—I'm busy changing history," Red said sarcastically.

"Remember what your mom said about being humiliated at *her first dance*? This must be what she meant!"

"And if someone did some horrible prank to her . . ." Red started connecting the dots.

"Maybe that's what turned her into a terrible dictator!" Chloe finished. The whole picture was finally coming together.

"That must be why the watch took us back to *this*

moment in time. It's before my mom turns into . . . my mom," Red said.

"Great! Now how do we fix it?" Chloe asked.

"By figuring out who's gonna do the prank that ruins her life." Red directed a suspicious glance around the room at the throng of students. *It could be any one of them . . .*

BRRRRIING!

The bell signaled the start of first period, and all the students darted out to make it to their classrooms in time.

"Late for class, ladies!" A man looked down from a walkway above them. He was older, maybe in his sixties, and wearing flowing professorial robes embroidered with sparkling swirls. "Stay right there . . ."

He rushed down to meet them, and Chloe tried to explain. "Actually, we're not students. Well, we are, but we think we've been sent—"

"Sent from . . . another place," Red cut in, glaring at Chloe. "We're transfer students!"

The man squinted at them over his glasses.

"I'm Principal Merlin, so I should have received papers . . ." he said. He opened his robe then, searching for the paperwork in pockets full of a bewildering assortment of odd pages and scrolls. "Let's see . . . No, that's not . . ."

He tossed the papers aside, and they magically vanished. Then he pulled out a burning candle. He vanished that next. "Oh, my, that's not safe at all." He sighed. "I'm sure it'll turn up eventually. Well, I founded this academy to be an educational institution for all." He eyed Chloe and, more important, her sword. "But you should know, we have a no-swords policy in the classroom."

He waved his wand, and Chloe's sword and scabbard disappeared in a flash of colorful light. She stared in amazement, delighted by his magic and only a little disappointed that he had stolen her sword.

"I've transported it to the Stardust Room, which will be your dormitory. We'll settle you in after school—but first let's get you to class. I teach Honors Alchemy in my office. Right this way . . ." He turned on his heel. "Oh . . . sorry . . . right *this* way. Follow me!"

Merlin conducted a small tour for Red and Chloe as he led them to class. In particular he pointed out the architectural features of the building.

"The marble of these archways was a gift from the kingdom of Camelot! And before you ask . . ."

Behind him, the girls hung back to have their own private conversation.

"What was that? The Auradon Code of Conduct *forbids* lying. Especially to teachers!" Chloe said.

"Good thing this isn't Auradon yet," said Red.

In front of them, Principal Merlin droned on. "There are no swords in *these* stones!" He was really making himself laugh.

They followed Merlin into another hallway.

"Here we are. Where's that blasted key?" He patted his robes before having an epiphany. "Ah!" he said, pulling a key out from behind his ear. He fitted it into the heavy wooden door, unlocked it, and led the two girls into what used to be, or what *would* be, Fairy Godmother's—no, *Uma's*—office. This office was full of Merlin's magical objects and was set up as a lab with workstations, each laid out with an assortment of ingredients. Chloe and Red took it all in. They'd never been around that kind of magic before.

"All right, class, let's get started! We've got two

new transfers here today, so let's at least pretend this is an honors class," Merlin said. His eyes scanned the room and lit up with inspiration as he chose two girls toward the back to assist his new transfers. "Bridget and Ella, split up and help these two get sorted, won't you?"

Red and Chloe couldn't contain their shock. Two girls stood at a lab table, chatting. They turned and smiled.

"Bridget?" Red asked.

"Mom!" Chloe exclaimed.

Chapter Eight

CHLOE: I guess now I can see if all of her "when I was your age" stories are even a little bit true . . .

Oh, no. Walk it back, Chloe.

"I mean . . . uh . . ." Chloe stammered, "Ella. Hi, nice to meet you!"

Stunned, she joined her new lab partner—the younger version of her mother—at her table. Ella was seventeen, not the elegant and strong princess she would become. Her tangled curls, fresh face, and hand-me-down clothes held together with patches were a strange sight for Chloe.

Ella gave Chloe a weird look. Probably because of the "mom" comment.

"Okay, new girl, let's dive in," Ella said.

Across the room, Red stood at a lab station with Bridget. She felt a mixture of confusion and terror. This sweet and smiley bubblegum-haired girl decked out in shades of pink couldn't possibly be the same person as Red's mother.

"So, wait—*you're* . . . Bridget? Bridget from Wonderland?" Red asked.

"Yep, that's me!" Bridget said.

Red couldn't help staring in disbelief.

Chloe and Ella were staring down a dark green seed pod.

Ella reached into the bucket on the table and grabbed the pod, squeezing it to extract a thick goo. Chloe watched, surprised by how easily her mom handled the disgusting plant. "You've just got to squeeze hard," Ella said casually.

"Oh, wow. These are gross," said Chloe, covering her nose with her shirt. They smelled *disgusting.*

"Come on, these pods don't drain themselves," Ella said.

"Could you pass me the griffin claw, please?" Bridget asked Red. "I gotta stir this up. I *love* your outfit, by the way."

"Why are you talking like that?" Red asked.

"Like what?"

"You just . . . sound different." Red was floored by the changes in this person she'd known her whole life.

"I'm not quite sure I—"

"No, it—it's me. I'm—You're—This is all just *a lot* to take in," Red said.

"Sorry, I just never had to . . . *Ew!*" The pod in Chloe's hands leaked goo everywhere.

Unimpressed, Ella looked Chloe over. Chloe dry-heaved.

"You okay?" Ella asked.

"Yeah, sorry, you're just . . . not what I was expecting," Chloe said.

Ella gave her a defensive look. "Why, you never worked with someone who's not *royalty*? Worried a commoner might rub off on you?"

"No!" Chloe cried. Ella looked skeptical. Chloe knew she was messing everything up.

Red and Bridget were doing slightly better at getting to know each other.

"How many kids were at your old school?"

"Uh . . . one," Red said. Just her.

"I was homeschooled, too! Until I came here.

Don't worry, you'll get used to it. Do you want a hug?" Bridget asked, moving in.

Red backed away. "Mmm, not really a hugger."

Bridget wasn't deterred. "I've got the perfect thing to make you feel better! I made 'em this morning." She leaned under the table and brought out a tray of bright pink cupcakes, each topped with a delicate pink feather.

Red paused, waiting for the joke. Her mother would never offer anyone a treat like that. She wouldn't offer *any* treats.

"Fabulous flamingo-feather cupcakes!" Bridget said proudly.

"Cupcakes?" Red asked, flabbergasted.

"Don't worry, they don't bite. Not like those gingerbread men I made last spring." Bridget giggled at the memory. "I won't be using *that* cookbook again."

Red stared for a moment, unable to believe this was really her mom. Then she tentatively took a bite of the delicious-looking cupcake. To her surprise, it was incredible. And also to her surprise, her long red-tipped nails had magically turned hot pink.

"Whoa! These *are* fabulous!" Red said, reaching for another. *That* was what her mother kept from her and all of Wonderland?

"Ah ah ah—just one, or there can be side effects. Now, ready to tackle the assignment?" Bridget asked.

"Why are you so *nice*?" Red asked, narrowing her eyes.

Bridget smiled and placed her hand on Red's arm. "You get more with sugar than salt," she said.

Red was dumbstruck by that answer. Who *was* this girl? And how had she turned into the Queen of Hearts?

But Bridget clearly intended to show Red what she meant. Once class was over, Bridget burst out of the office, carrying her cupcakes with her while Red, Chloe, and Ella followed. The other students from their class trailed after the group.

In the quad, students ate lunch with their friend groups and Bridget carried her tray, dropping off a cupcake with each student she passed. As they tried her cupcakes, they transformed in their own unique ways. Someone's tights turned bright pink. Then someone else's pants! A pair of sneakers! A hat!

Everyone who ate a cupcake pulled a sweet dance move. It seemed like Bridget knew exactly how to brighten the entire school's mood.

Continuing her mission to make sure everyone got a treat, Bridget approached Fay, who was sitting by herself, looking stressed. Fay took a big bite of a cupcake and her magic wand transformed.

Bridget smiled and moved on to Merlin Academy's resident inseparable couple, Jasmine and Aladdin. Next Bridget called out to Charming—Chloe's dad!

All four of the girls dodged out of the way as the young and gorgeous version of Chloe's dad zoomed by on a skateboard, with his shoulder-length hair tucked under his helmet. He skated in a circle and snagged a cupcake. He dug in as he flipped, and in midair, his board turned bright pink. Red liked his style.

"Okay," Red said coyly. For an Auradon guy, he was pretty cute . . .

"That's my dad!" Chloe said.

"Oh . . ." Red said sheepishly.

Red caught up to Bridget, who was still handing out cupcakes. "So you're friends with everyone?"

"Oh, gosh no, my only friend is Ella. But with time and a few more treats, they will be!" Bridget said.

Out of Bridget's view, Ella widened her eyes for Red and Chloe's benefit, clearly saying, *No, they won't.*

But the moment was quickly interrupted by the arrival of the VKs, tumbling into the courtyard in a riot of sound. Red could barely believe that there had been a time *before* Queen Mal and King Ben when VKs and AKs went to school together. This looked like madness so far.

The first one to step up and introduce himself was Hook, a preening rich kid with an earring and a shiny hook where his left hand should have been. Following Hook was Morgie, son of Morgana le Fay. He was a blond charmer wearing serpent-green silks. Hades, a fiery bad boy in a leather motorcycle jacket, and his girlfriend, Maleficent, wearing a horned headpiece, joined them next. Last, Uliana, the younger sister of Ursula, arrived with all eight of her wicked tentacles and a seashell necklace on display. Uliana's tentacle shot out and snagged a cupcake from Bridget's tray, shocking Red and Chloe.

"Thanks . . ." Uliana said.

"Oh, sure! Of course! Happy to—" Bridget started.

Another one of Uliana's tentacles slithered around and stole the entire tray.

"For *all*. I mean, flamingo feathers are, like, rare, right?" Uliana asked, her tentacle holding the tray much higher than Bridget could reach.

Ella stepped up defiantly. "Hey! Give that back to her!"

"I'm sorry?" Uliana said mockingly. "I don't speak peasant-girl. Love your outfit, by the way. It's so . . . put-together."

With another tentacle, Uliana pulled the threads on Ella's patched shirt and left it tattered and torn. The VKs laughed, especially Morgie and Hook, who were desperate to win Uliana's favor.

Uliana put on an innocent face and used her magic power to mimic Bridget's voice perfectly. With her magic shell necklace glowing, she said, "My name's Bridget, and I have to bribe people to be my friend with treats, 'cause I'm such a loner."

Chloe picked up a bat someone had left behind

and wielded it like a sword. She threatened Uliana: "Hey! The Code of Conduct prohibits theft *and* bullying!"

Hook stepped in and wrapped Chloe's bat-sword in his hook, neutralizing her.

"Easy, lass. I don't know where you come from, but here we don't fight until after school. Meet me then," Hook said. He leaned in, smitten despite her obvious disgust.

Chloe pushed him away. "You wouldn't stand a chance," she said to him.

He just laughed as he backed away.

Undaunted, Red stepped up to Uliana next. "Listen, squid-face. Give the cupcakes back—or I'll rip that magic tongue out of your throat."

Uliana smirked. "Girl, I only wanted the feathers." Her tentacle plucked the feathers off all the cupcakes. "You can have the rest," she said.

But then she whipped the tray at the ground, and the cupcakes splattered onto the hard stones at their feet. Uliana grinned and then opened her mouth, ready to drop the feathers inside.

"Wait! That's too many—" Bridget started.

It was too late. Uliana popped the feathers into her mouth and swallowed them whole. Instantly, her lips and eyelashes turned bright pink.

"You shouldn't have done that," Bridget said sadly.

"You are just jealous of the fabulosity," Uliana said, pulling out a mirror. She puckered her lips, admiring her reflection. "You can't handle my—"

SQUAAAWK!

A wild birdcall involuntarily erupted from Uliana's mouth. Her friends stared at her, confused.

"What was—" Uliana started.

SQUAAAWK! She let out another bird sound, and pink feathers sprouted all over her body, popping out one by one.

"You all right, Uli?" Hook asked cautiously. "You're lookin' a little . . . pink."

"What's happening to me? Get them—"

BRAAAH! Another loud bird sound was released from her mouth, and Uliana fell to the ground. From all across the lawn, students converged, staring at her. Flamingo Uliana looked around, panicked and embarrassed. She tried to speak but could only squawk.

"Someone help her!" Fay shouted.

"Yeah, someone should help her . . ." drawled Hades, making no move to do so.

Morgie tried to get her back on her feet, but she pushed him off.

And when Uli looked up, ready to snap at him, everyone saw that she had grown a massive pink beak.

Flamingo Uliana glanced around frantically before her gaze locked on Bridget. *RAAAAH!* She ran at Bridget. Bridget tried to escape, but Uliana pursued her relentlessly, all the way to a fountain.

"Bridget! Bridget!" Ella cried.

Uliana rushed around the fountain, nearly catching Bridget, until Ella stepped in and hip-checked her. Uliana toppled sideways and splashed into the fountain. The crowd of students watched as she floundered in the water.

Bridget stared, speechless. Ella coolly led her by the elbow out of harm's way.

After a moment, Uliana thrashed up to her feet, back in human form and soaking wet. Even though the magical transformation had worn off for Uliana *and* the student body, Uliana was mortified at everyone laughing at her. She had never been so humiliated in her life.

"Where's Bridget?" she growled.

Red stood in shock next to Chloe. "So . . . pretty sure we just found out who's gonna do the prank?" Red asked.

"I dunno, maybe that wasn't *so* bad?" Chloe said.

A sopping wet Uliana screeched in anger. "I will *destroy* her," Uliana vowed.

Red shot Chloe a disbelieving look. It couldn't have been clearer than *that*.

"Maybe it was," conceded Chloe.

"Tell Bridget this isn't over!" cried Uliana.

Chapter Nine

RED: If only this little punk Uliana could see what Bridget was going to turn into! She would never mess with her again. But come to think of it, I'd never heard of Uliana before . . . Maybe my mom *did* show her who's boss . . .

The girls caught up to their mothers inside.

"How's Uli doing?" Bridget asked. "I feel so terrible . . . I should go apologize—"

"Don't!" Ella said. "She did it to herself. And it serves her right. She's always bullying us."

The door opened, stalling the conversation, and Prince Charming walked in.

"Ella, that was amazing. You ladies bested Uliana! I don't think anyone's ever done that before. That makes you braver than I am. And I'm a prince!" He turned to Red and Chloe. "Though I don't really like to push the royal angle."

"Yet you always find a way," Ella said stiffly.

Charming grinned at her attitude and turned once more to Red and Chloe.

"You're the new girls, right? I'm Charming."

"That's debatable," Ella said.

He ignored her dig and continued speaking to Red and Chloe.

"And you guys picked the right time to show up, because . . . it's Castlecoming week!" he said.

He tried to catch Ella's eye, but no luck. She seemed to be intentionally avoiding his gaze.

"Castlecoming is an outdated, elitist tradition," Ella said.

"Wait, so . . . does that mean you're not . . ." Charming started.

"Squeezing into a super-expensive dress and painful shoes? No thanks," Ella said.

Charming tried to hide his disappointment. "Right. Well . . . if you happen to change your mind, I'll see ya there."

He turned and took off down the hall. Ella watched him, her expression unreadable.

"Hey, Ella, he seemed very interested in *your* plans for the festival," Chloe said. "Was I sensing some chemistry?"

"Uh, no. Okay, yeah, everyone loves him. And sure, he's gorgeous and he seems nice, but you know how royalty is." She quickly corrected herself. "Except you, B. You're different."

Chloe stared at her mother in disbelief. How her parents had ever ended up together was starting to seem like a mystery to her.

Bridget sighed longingly. "I just wish someone was that interested in going with *me*. Everyone already has plans, so . . ." she explained to Red.

Ella looked at her with a sly smile. "Bridget, will you go to Castlecoming with me?"

"But you just said . . ." Bridget started.

"I despise everything it stands for. But if we go as friends, maybe it won't be *totally* awful."

Ecstatic, Bridget squealed. "We have to go try on dresses right now. We only have two days!" She spun into Ella's arms.

"I can't. I have to get back home. But maybe later?"

"Okay," said Bridget, with a smile still stuck on her face. Nothing was going to ruin her excitement.

Bridget squeezed Ella again, then hurried up the stairs to the dorms above.

"I'd better get home," Ella said. She made her way outside, leaving Red and Chloe to share a look.

They turned on their heels and walked deeper into the first floor of the building. "Two days until my mom gets pranked," Red said.

"That's not enough time!" Chloe said, panicked.

"It's gonna have to be," Red said.

Searching for a private place to talk, the girls

headed through an opening in the foyer to an empty music room.

Red, agitated, moved through the space with Chloe next to her. "I can't believe my mom was so . . . *sweet*."

Red passed by an organ and dragged her hand across its keys, setting it off. Chloe hurried to muffle the noise with her own hands as best she could.

"Tell me about it!" Chloe said. "My mom's supposed to be the most perfect, gracious queen ever. Ella seems like she can't even stand royalty."

"Yeah—and you know the craziest thing of all?" Red asked.

"They were best friends," both girls cried at the same time.

They stood in mutually stunned silence for a moment. It was so *weird* when they were on the same page.

"Okay, now the question is . . . how do we stop Uliana before Castlecoming?" Chloe said.

"First we have to figure out what she's planning. Bugs in Bridget's dress? Or something with snakes?

Ugh, so many good options," Red mused. She knocked her hand into a set of hanging chimes, and the noise echoed in the empty music room. Once again, Chloe rushed to silence them.

"So let's find out more about Uliana," Chloe said. "You think my mom might know?"

"Maybe. Plus, she's closest to Bridget. So she'll know her weaknesses—and exactly how to stab her in the back," Red said. She lifted a mallet, ready to bang it against a drum, but Chloe caught her arm and gently stopped her.

Chloe squinted at her with confusion and curiosity. "You have some serious intimacy issues."

Away from Auradon Prep, a sprawling manor that clearly once had been very grand and loved now sat covered in thick vines and shuttered by dark, filthy windows.

Red and Chloe made their way closer to the house, running through all they'd learned during their wild day at Merlin Academy.

"So, wait, that girl Uliana is Uma's . . . aunt?" asked Red.

"Remind me never to get sent to the principal's office," said Chloe. She looked around at their surprising surroundings. "Is this the right house?"

"This place could use a paint job," said Red. "Or a bulldozer."

But they stepped up to the large and intimidating front door anyway, and after a beat, Chloe knocked.

Ella answered, holding a duster and looking *very* displeased to see them. Behind her, the entryway was in disarray. Ella tried her best to block their view of the mess, but it was too late.

"Uh, what are you guys doing here?" Ella asked, frantic.

"We came to see you!" Chloe said cheerfully.

But Ella wasn't able to respond before a window opened above and Ella's severe-looking evil stepmother poked her head out.

The woman shouted, "Who's there?"

"Just some girls from school!" Ella yelled up to her.

"Get back to work, or no supper!" her stepmother reminded her.

With a *ka-thunk*, her stepmother shut the window and disappeared back inside the house. Ella cringed, painfully embarrassed to have had anyone see how her stepmother treated her.

"Sorry, my stepmom is . . ." she started.

"A total witch?" Red suggested. "I get it. My mom never let me have friends over. Or *have* friends."

"Really?" Ella brightened slightly at Red's words, feeling better now that she knew she was around someone who could relate.

Chloe was shocked to see that Red was having an easier time bonding with her mom than she was.

"Okay. You guys can stay, but you have to help with my chores," Ella said.

The girls followed her inside, surprised to see just how cluttered the house was.

Ella hauled a bucket and some scrub brushes into the massive tiled entryway of the manor. The floors were caked with dirt and grime.

She handed Chloe a mop and Red a duster. "There you go," she said. "The floor needs mopping, and over there needs dusting."

"You do all the housework?" Chloe asked seriously.

"Yeah, all on me," Ella said.

Red set off to the spot Ella had pointed at, and Chloe tried to get to work.

"Am I doing this right?" she asked. But as soon as she did, she slipped on the wet floor in her glass boots.

"I think it's time to lose the glass shoes," Red said.

"But these were from my mom. They were a reward," Chloe whined.

"A reward for what?" Red asked.

"For volunteering, being good at school, and . . . being a good person."

"Does it really count as being a good person if you're getting a reward for it?"

Chloe stopped in her tracks. She had never thought of it that way. She'd never had to question whether she truly was a good person. Before she could spiral too deeply into her thoughts, Red changed the subject, ready to get down to business.

"So, Ella, that thing with Uliana at school . . . pretty wild, huh?"

"Seriously. She's as bad as Ursula," Ella said. At Red's questioning look, she continued.

"Uliana's older sister. The worst bully this school has ever seen. One time she turned all the freshmen into frogs. And now Uliana thinks she has to be even meaner to try and live up to her reputation," Ella said.

"But why does Uliana have it out for *Bridget*? Bridget is so nice," Chloe said.

"Exactly," Red said. "Bullies love an easy target. Bridget is weak."

Ella scoffed. "You think Bridget is weak?"

Confused, Red paused.

"Uliana is mean to everyone. Most people just stay out of her way. But no matter how nasty Uliana gets, Bridget keeps trying to be friends. That's what Uliana can't stand," Ella said.

"You're saying Bridget is strong because she's *nice*?" Red asked. The idea went against everything her mother had taught her.

"Bridget is the strongest person I know. She's kind even when people are awful to her. You know how hard that is?" Ella said.

Red stopped working then, totally shaken by the revelation. What were the chances when that day had started that Cinderella herself would be teaching Red to see the idea of strength in a whole new light? The thought was laughable.

"I . . . never thought about it." Red shifted gears then. "Say we wanted to find Uliana . . . Where do you think she'd be?"

"Probably the Black Lagoon. That's where the VKs hang out."

Lost in her thoughts, Chloe turned around, absentmindedly knocking over a vase. It crashed to the floor. All the girls froze in place, not daring to breathe. Maybe it would be okay. Maybe no one had heard. But then, from a distant room, a bone-chilling shriek of rage filled the space.

"What . . . was . . . that*?"* Ella's evil stepmother yelled.

"Nothing, Stepmother," Ella called back.

"Quick, sweep it into the fireplace and she'll

never know," Red said, motioning toward the hearth.

"It was an honest mistake," said Chloe.

But Ella frantically started sweeping the shards of the vase into the fireplace anyway.

Ella's stepmother rushed into the room, a scowl already on her face.

Chloe stepped forward, ready to take the blame. "It was my fault. But I'm very sorry, and it won't happen again."

After Chloe's confession, Ella's evil stepmother zoned in on the fireplace and spotted the broken shards. She was livid, not at all understanding like Chloe thought she would be.

To Ella, her stepmother said, "You let a stranger into my house and let her break my beautiful things? Unacceptable."

"But . . . I said I was sorry," Chloe said, shocked.

"Sorry doesn't buy me a new vase!" She turned to Ella. "You can kiss Castlecoming goodbye. You are grounded." She reached out and touched the frayed edge of Ella's sleeve. "And tonight you can sleep in the barn."

She marched out, calling for Ella's stepsisters,

Anastasia and Drizella, as she did. "Anastasia, Drizella—where are you? It's time for your dress fitting!"

"Ella, I'm so sorry," Chloe said, astounded by what had just happened.

"Sorry doesn't get me un-grounded before Castlecoming. Next time don't be such a *princess*."

"But that was so . . . *unfair*!" Chloe said.

Ella whirled on Chloe then, finally out of patience with the annoying new girl. "You know what's unfair? My mom died when I was so little I barely even remember her. My dad got remarried . . . but then he died, too. Since then, this is the only family I've known. And no matter how good I am, they still treat me like dirt. So, yeah, it's unfair . . . because *life* isn't fair. Just leave."

Chloe was speechless. Irritated, Ella started picking up the broken shards. Chloe wanted to help, but Red ushered her away.

"We should give her a little time," Red said.

So Chloe let Red turn them back toward Merlin Academy.

Chapter Ten

CHLOE: I share everything with my mom. She's my best friend. I can't believe I didn't know this about her. What else has she kept hidden from me? And once we go after the VKs, will I even make it back to the present to ask her?

Back at Merlin Academy, a hushed darkness had fallen over campus. It was late—later than Red and Chloe had any business being out walking through the woods.

Red pushed past bare branches of dying trees

and emerged on the bank of the swampy lagoon, leaving Chloe to catch up behind her. They surveyed the area. There were no VKs present. There was nothing but an occasional bubble rising to the surface of the water and popping with a sickly squelch.

Why was the place so deserted?

Suddenly, voices approached from the nearby woods.

"I thought you were a beautiful flamingo, Uli," Hook joked.

"It's the VKs," Red whispered.

Red and Chloe ducked to hide just in time as the VKs tore through the trees. Uliana was fuming, with her VK crew trailing behind her. One thing was clear from their conversation: they were dead set on getting the perfect revenge on Bridget.

When they got to the edge of the Black Lagoon, Uliana raised the seashell on her necklace to her lips and blew a haunting note. The shell glowed, and the black pool rippled outward in cascading waves. The waters before them began to churn. Red and Chloe glanced at each other, dreading what might happen.

Suddenly, Uliana's lair rose from the murky depths, revealing the location of her hideout: inside the colossal remains of some petrified sea creature. The floating fortress came to a rest in the middle of the lagoon, with dark water streaming off its giant spiked spine. Stepping stones drifted to the surface one by one, silently creating a path from the shore to the mouth of the lair. Through the open jaws, a demon glow beckoned. Uliana and the VKs danced their way across the stones giddily. As they crossed, the ridge of something black and serpentine broke the surface of the water and then, just as quickly, slithered back into the darkness. Red and Chloe watched the VKs disappear into the belly of the beast and took two deep breaths.

Uliana stormed inside her secret hideout. The interior matched her foul mood: A hazy neon light swirled around the walls, made of ancient bones. Seaweed clung to every surface. In the center of the lair sat a large black cauldron, ready for evil deeds. Uliana's tentacles lifted her into the air as she turned to her minions to ask if they had any suggestions for her revenge.

Hook suggested Bridget walk the plank.

Maleficent suggested Uliana prick Bridget with a thousand thorns.

Hades suggested burning Bridget to a crisp—and Morgie agreed.

But Uliana shook her head, feeling like she was surrounded by unimaginative morons. *No,* she thought, *these won't do*. She'd need help from the cauldron itself to find the right recipe for her revenge. At her command, Hades snapped his fingers to start the blazing fire beneath the cauldron.

Outside, Red and Chloe climbed the exterior of the lair, clinging to spiked protrusions. They carefully crawled along the spine and then came to a stop and clawed a hole through the lair's slimy walls. From there, they could peer down into the VK hideout and overhear the plans being made.

Uliana leaned over the cauldron as it glowed and steamed. The vapors took the shape of an ethereal image: a leather-bound book, enclosed with a silver clasp.

"What's this? A book? That's it? I asked for a painful punishment!" Uliana cried.

But then the book rotated to reveal its cover. In big lettering, it said *The Sorcerer's Cookbook*. Right away, Uli could see the plan: she'd trick Bridget with something that would embarrass her as much as Bridget had embarrassed Uli. All she needed was this one little book.

Pumped, the VKs rushed across the stepping stones outside the lair, determined to find the cookbook that would help them bake up something not so sweet for Bridget. Uliana made it to the bank last and raised her shell to blow one eerie note. Then she looked at her VKs.

"We'll bake our own treat . . . and turn her into a giant monster." Her eyes glinted as she turned and led her VKs back to the school.

As soon as the VKs had retreated far enough into the woods, Red and Chloe scrambled, dropping from the hideous entrance onto the first stepping stone. Red led the way, hurrying back across the lagoon, but slammed to a stop when a dark shape rippled the water ahead of them. It moved incredibly fast just below the surface, and another splash alerted Chloe to what they were dealing with.

"What was that?" asked Red.

As she spoke, the floating stones began to sink one by one. Red raced ahead, making it to safety, with Chloe right behind as the dark shape of an eel closed in on her. Just as the last stepping stone sank beneath her foot, Chloe leapt and flopped onto the shore. She was exhaling, relieved, when suddenly the eel erupted from the water and lunged onto the bank after her. It snapped its jaws at Chloe's feet—and when Chloe looked to Red for help, Red completely froze. Was she really not going to help Chloe? After all they'd been through together?

Chloe kicked at the eel, terrified, and clutched the roots of a nearby tree for purchase as the eel tugged her down closer to the water's edge. Snapping out of her trance, Red grabbed a branch, roughly the same size as her trusty croquet mallet, from a withered tree. When the eel lunged at Chloe again, its razor-sharp teeth about to clamp down on her, Red smashed the eel with a baseball swing across its jaw. Red spun and hit it again, then raised the branch and walloped the eel on its head. *Yes!* A triple combo, Red's signature move.

The stunned eel sank into the depths of the lagoon, and Red pulled Chloe farther from the water. Both girls caught their breath in silence, processing what had just happened.

"You okay?" Red finally asked.

"Yeah . . . thanks," said Chloe.

Red shrugged nonchalantly. "You're no good to me as fish food."

Betraying her cool demeanor, Red playfully whacked her on the shoulder.

Chloe broke the moment. "We can still stop them before Castlecoming, but that means—"

"We've got a book to find," Red finished.

Chapter Eleven

CHLOE: I really like Red's mom—well, I like her now, or I guess I should say, *then*. Maybe if we fix things, we can save more than just my mom. Maybe we can save Red's relationship with the Queen, and our moms' friendship, too.

Back at the dormitory, the girls did their best to relax in their temporary room. The quarters were spacious, with two canopy beds, where the girls had tossed their jackets. Chloe paced around the room, processing the new information she had on her mother.

"Where could that book be?" she wondered aloud. "Who could we ask? Not Ella. I still can't believe how awful her family was to her. I just don't understand how someone grows up like *that* and turns into . . . my mom! How can one person change so much?"

Red was lying on her back on top of her bed. "Tell me about it. My mom changed her entire personality. It's like everything she does now is to make people afraid of her and hide the fact that she used to actually be nice," Red said.

"Well, whatever we do, we have to make sure that she stays that way. My mom's life depends on it." When Red gave Chloe a confused look, Chloe continued. "Think about it. What if your mom had grown up to be like Bridget?"

"You mean completely clueless?"

"Or kind, generous, and openhearted," Chloe said. "She wouldn't have become a tyrant!"

Red slowly realized the ramifications of a Bridget

who never turned evil. Obviously, it would have helped the entire world, but the change it would have caused in Red's own little world was almost unimaginable. *Almost.* "I could eat what I want. And sleep when I want. And wear what I want. And be what I want. I'd be free of my mom. And her rules. And her judgy face . . ."

"She might not be judgy at all," said Chloe. "She might be loving, and kind."

"It doesn't matter," Red said, shaking her head. "It's not like I actually care about that."

But the truth was that Red desperately wanted that. She just couldn't admit it to herself—let alone another person. She hated to acknowledge it, but she was starting to long for a future where her mom was more like Bridget.

But Chloe wasn't letting her off easy. "I think . . . maybe you do." She went to her jacket and pulled the watch out of its pocket. "What if the watch brought us back here because what you really want is . . . a mom—who can love you the way that you are? A mom more like Bridget?"

It wasn't even a question. Red's armor cracked

then and there. She tried to hold back the emotion, but a tear formed in the corner of her eye and betrayed her.

Chloe had seen into her heart. Because Chloe was starting to know Red all too well, she also knew to crack a joke so Red could carefully tuck her feelings away for the time being.

"She'd probably still be making cupcakes!" Chloe said with a laugh.

But joke aside, the comment sparked something in Red—an idea.

"Wait," she said slowly. "That's it. We should ask Bridget about the cookbook!"

The next morning, the sun rose over Auradon Prep as Bridget worked through a card trick in her dorm. She wore long-sleeved pajamas and a pair of old-school over-ear headphones.

"Hmm . . . perfect!" she said, pleased. She had mastered the trick.

She was interrupted by a knock on the door. Red and Chloe were standing on the other side.

"Hey, guys! I'm just practicing my signature dance for Castlecoming. I call it the Shuffle of Love," Bridget said.

She demonstrated it: the Shuffle of Love was a routine where she shuffled a deck of cards and added some really cool tricks and dance moves. For the big finale, she tossed the deck down and tried to kick it back up, but the cards scattered everywhere.

"Ah, I keep messing up the last bit. But it's okay! I'll get there," she said. "Let me clean this up real quick."

As she scooped up the cards, Red and Chloe looked around her room. It was decorated in shades of pink, with neon lights and lava lamps, and there was even an entire corner for her baking supplies.

"Wow, your room. It's so wonderful!" Chloe said.

"Oh, yeah, thanks! It reminds me of home," Bridget said.

Red gawked, trying to mentally link Bridget's home with her own.

"Where I come from, there's a rule against . . . *all* of this," Red said.

"Who's against fun?" Bridget asked.

"Our queen. Aka my mom," Red said.

"Oh," said Bridget.

"She also hates my style, the way I think, you know—everything about me," Red added.

"I'm sorry, Red. I can't imagine having a mom like that," Bridget said.

Red couldn't believe she was having this conversation *about* her mom *with* her mom. She felt her heart breaking just a bit.

"She's the only one I've ever known," Red said quietly.

"Well, if I was your mom, I'd *love* to have a daughter who thinks for herself," Bridget said. She reached out and gave Red a reassuring touch.

Those were the words Red had always wanted to hear from her mom, but they meant almost nothing coming from *this* version of her mom. Chloe gave Red an *I told you so* eyebrow raise, but Red looked away, her emotions swirling. Her eyes landed on a familiar gold compact on Bridget's desk.

"Is that . . . the Looking Glass?" Red asked.

"Oh, yeah! You've heard of it?" Bridget said.

"Uh . . . I've read about it," Red lied quickly.

"It was a gift. Been in the Wonderland royal line for ages."

"What's it do?" Chloe asked.

"It shows you the future!" Bridget said.

Nervous and curious, Red asked, "Have you . . . looked?"

"Oh no, no no no! I love surprises!" Bridget said cheerfully. "Why would I want to spoil the future? I'm sure it'll be wonderful."

Bridget smiled, and it was clear she was daydreaming of all the possibilities her future held. Red and Chloe weren't so hopeful.

"*Sure.* Anyway, we were hoping that you might be able to help us find a cookbook," Red said, pulling Bridget's attention to the reason they had stopped by.

"Then you've got the right girl! I have every cookbook ever."

"Even *The Sorcerer's Cookbook*?" Red asked.

"Hmm . . . let me look." Bridget popped her headphones back on and danced across the room to a shelf overflowing with cookbooks. She slid her finger across the titles on her bookshelf.

While Bridget was distracted, Red sneakily swiped the Looking Glass.

"What are you doing?" Chloe hissed.

"Checking how things are going back home," Red said, flipping open the compact.

Chloe watched in awe as the mirrored surface swirled and became a screen, showing them their own time:

In the school courtyard, Wonderland flags hung from the stone walls and the Queen of Hearts had set up a command center. A huge map of Auradon, showing all the kingdoms in the land, was spread across the floor. A red queen chess piece had been placed on every territory except for one: Cinderellasburg, which was still marked by a blue knight.

All eyes turned on a pair of card soldiers as they dragged a prisoner into the courtyard. It was King Charming, Chloe's dad.

"Charming. Nice to see you again," the Queen of Hearts said.

On the map, she knocked aside the blue knight

with another red queen chess piece. Her takeover was complete.

"Where is she? Where's Cinderella?" King Charming cried.

"Why—are you looking for these?" the Queen asked sarcastically, gleefully dangling Cinderella's glass shoes before him.

Then she tossed them and watched as they shattered.

"Not so funny now, am I?" she asked.

The king fell to his knees, gathering up the shards of glass. "No . . . no. No!"

In the past, Red clamped the compact shut. After an entire lifetime of dealing with her mother, Red was somehow still shocked by her behavior. Maybe she had gotten too used to the niceness Bridget doled out to everyone.

"Okay, so . . . not good," Red said.

Chloe's lip quivered. She was on the verge of tears. Red squeezed her shoulder, comforting her. Bridget stopped grooving in front of the bookshelf and turned back to the girls, oblivious to what they had just seen. She removed her headphones.

"That's weird. I thought I had them all. Except the banned ones," she said.

"Where would we find a banned one?" Red asked.

"We don't," Bridget said, scandalized. "They're dangerous! That's why Principal Merlin locked them up in his office—and enchanted them so no trouble-makers can get their hands on them . . ." She wandered off.

Red and Chloe shared a look.

Reeling, the girls returned to their room to figure out their next step.

"Now that we know where the book is, I think the solution is clear," Chloe said, resolute.

"For sure. There's only one option," Red agreed.

"It's time to tell Principal Merlin. We need to come clean. He can help us."

Red's eyes bugged. "No! *Help us?* You think he's just gonna hand over a banned book because we ask him?"

"Do you have a better idea?" Chloe asked.

"Yeah! We do it ourselves. We break in and steal it! That's what Uliana's gonna do. Unless we get there first."

Chloe scoffed. *Of course that's where Red's mind goes.*

"You want to break in . . . to the principal's office? It's enchanted—it's dangerous! And Castlecoming is tomorrow. We only have one shot to get this right. And your idea is to steal?"

"And your plan is to go tell the teacher? You're such a goody-goody," Red said.

"I'd rather be a goody-goody than a bad person," Chloe said stiffly.

All her life, Red had balanced being herself and being what her mother wanted her to be. She knew she wasn't perfect—in fact, she didn't want to *be* perfect—but for Chloe to call her a bad person after her years of struggling . . . it hurt. Red lashed back. "You sound like your mom."

"Thank you!" Chloe said.

"And how'd that work out for her?" Red asked. It was a low blow, but she couldn't help feeling that

Chloe needed to hear it—even if she didn't want to.

Chloe's eyes narrowed. "Wow. You know, you *are* evil. Just like *your* mom."

The Looking Glass's vision of Red ruling Auradon beside the Queen of Hearts flashed back into Red's mind.

"Maybe. But I'm gonna get us out of here," she said.

Without another word, she stormed out and slammed the door, leaving Chloe alone and fuming. Chloe knew exactly who she'd go to for help with this problem if she were back home, in her own time: her best friend and role model. But what was she supposed to do when that person currently thought she was a spoiled brat?

Chapter Twelve

RED: If you ask me, Chloe has a personality only a mother could love. So it makes sense that she would be desperate enough to go crawling back to find her mom, even if she's totally unwelcome at Ella's house.

Chloe decided that coming off as annoying was worth it if she might receive some good advice. So against her better judgment, she ended up back at Ella's evil stepmother's château.

But when Chloe arrived, she found a scene she

never could've imagined her mom in. Hunched over, sweaty, and filthy, Ella plunged her hands into the dirt of the circular garden bed surrounding the fountain at the front of the home and tugged free a large gnarly weed. The dilapidated fountain hadn't worked in ages and was full of sludge and debris.

Chloe walked up and tried to appear friendly, even though she was irritated with Red and nervous that her mother wouldn't want her there.

"Hey! Can I talk to you about something?" she asked Ella.

Ella looked up from her work briefly and then went back to weeding.

Chloe gave in; she could've guessed that Ella would react that way. "Normally I talk to my mom when I have a problem, but she's . . . she's far away right now, so . . ." Chloe shrugged like, *Here I am*. Ella just stared, but Chloe pressed on. "Say you have a friend—or, not a friend, but someone you know—who's a bad person."

"How do you know they're a bad person?" Ella asked.

"'Cause she says so herself!"

"Bad people don't think they're bad. Trust me—I live with one," Ella said, jerking her head toward the château.

"Okay—but what if they keep pushing you to do something bad, but they say it's for a good reason?"

Ella considered the question and then handed Chloe a trowel, pointing to the overgrown garden bed. Chloe tried to do as instructed, but she was terrible at it. She jabbed at the ground with the point of her trowel. Ella demonstrated, grabbing a weed by the base and yanking it out, root and all. While they worked, Ella explained her perspective on Chloe's problem: that sometimes a bad action could be done for a good cause. Chloe was shocked to hear those words from her mother's mouth—almost as shocked as she was when she finally yanked out the giant weed she'd been pulling on and fell backward onto her behind.

She followed Ella to a garden shed, where Ella threw open the door, bathing the tools and cobwebs inside in sunlight. Chloe struggled to keep up, unused to all this manual labor and grappling with what Ella was telling her. Chloe had always believed that if she was good, good things would come to her. But Ella had brought up the broken vase from the last time Chloe had shown up at her stepmother's château: sometimes good people did less-than-perfect things, even if they didn't mean to.

Chloe contemplated all this as the two carried on, turning their attention to the fountain itself. They bailed out nasty bits of trash one at a time and got to scrubbing the dingy old stone. That place was starting to shine thanks to their work.

Chloe questioned Ella: How far was too far? How much should she compromise?

Ella told her in no uncertain terms: she would do whatever her heart told her was right, especially if it was for someone she loved. Or . . . to save someone's life.

Chloe flashed back—or forward—to her mother standing up to the Queen of Hearts in the courtyard. She had to do *something* to save her mom's life. She couldn't play it clean, because the situation they were in wasn't neat and tidy. She'd have to get her hands dirty.

Chloe and Ella had one more task to tackle: unsticking an old handwheel. Eventually, they got it to turn and—*whoosh!*—water erupted from the jets and arced through the air, filling the fountain. Success!

With the garden bursting with colorful blooms and the fountain in much better shape, Chloe, brimming with emotion, looked at her mom.

"I knew you'd have the answer," Chloe said. "Thank you."

And then Chloe took off, back toward the school. Ella stood there, watching Chloe leave, absolutely puzzled by the comment.

Chapter Thirteen

CHLOE: There's no point in being good just to say you're good—not if it's not helping anyone. And I know a lot of people who need some major help. Like all of Auradon!

Outside the walls of Merlin Academy, Uli and her band of VKs huddled under a tree for protection from the rain. Hook, with his signature smirk in place, looked through a pair of binoculars.

"The coast is clear," he said.

But Uli stopped him before he could move. "Not yet," she warned him.

She was right to be cautious—because inside Merlin Academy, a hooded figure approached the heavy wooden door to the principal's office. Red pulled out an improvised lockpick and made quick work of it. As she was about to open the door, she heard footsteps. She whirled around—

And found Chloe.

Chloe had changed into a vintage Merlin Academy tourney uniform, and the midnight-blue dress dotted with gold stars made her look like a true hero. With her sword strapped to her waist and her gloves covering her hands, she was clearly ready for action and reporting for duty.

"What're *you* doing here?" Red asked, ready for a fight.

"Getting my hands dirty," Chloe said simply.

"You're gonna break into the principal's office?" Red couldn't keep a smile from stretching across her face.

"It's for a good cause," Chloe said, resolute.

"And you're already justifying your crimes? Love it," Red said approvingly.

Chloe huffed a laugh, letting the comment go. They both headed into the office, swinging the door almost all the way shut behind them.

Outside the building, Uli and her band of VKs lay in wait.

Uliana turned to Morgie and gave him a flirtatious look. "Morgie, honey, you keep lookout, okay? If you see Merlin coming, give a signal."

"Should I do a wolf howl? Or, like, a dog howl? I can do different dogs . . ." Morgie started, but the other VKs were already heading toward the school.

The high-ceilinged chamber was stuffed with a massive bookshelf, a medieval fireplace big enough to stand inside, and shelves full of artifacts. At the center sat Merlin's desk—a round table, aptly, with a crest inscribed in its stone surface. A dozen swords were inlaid in the crest, pointing toward the middle like the spokes of a wheel.

The girls approached the bookshelf and scanned the titles. Red started up the ladder leaning against the shelves.

"Wait, I think I see it!" said Chloe. "The big one, with the claws!"

She pointed, and Red's eyes narrowed at a sinister-looking leather-bound book with *The Sorcerer's Cookbook* on thc spine. It was way over, out of reach.

Neither of them noticed that the stone owls standing sentry on Merlin's fireplace mantel blinked . . . and opened their glowing eyes.

As Red pushed herself as far as she could get, trying to make contact with the book's spine, the stone owls nodded down at the round table in the center of the room. The twelve swords from the crest in the round table dislodged from the stone and magically floated up into the air. Red noticed a shadow falling over the books in front of her, and she looked back.

"Oh boy," she said. Understatement of the century.

Suddenly, one of the swords flew right at her. Red let go of the ladder and slid down to the floor, dodging it. As more swords began to attack, Chloe pulled Red out of the way and drew her own blade.

"Move!" Chloe cried. Swords flew from all sides.

The stone owls prepared to take flight. One flapped its huge wings, flew into the unlit fireplace, and ascended straight up the chimney.

"Oh, no," Chloe moaned. "It's going to tell Merlin!"

But they couldn't worry about that right then: the swords were still coming straight for them.

Chloe and Red fled in opposite directions, with Red improvising a weapon out of a floor candelabra to defend herself.

Outside, Morgie sat up at his post . . . and watched the owl fly from Merlin's office.

Inside, Red ducked behind a vertical beam just in time for a sword to skewer it. The next attack forced Red to a spiral staircase, and when she made it to the balcony above it, she got a good visual of Chloe knocking swords every which way below.

"Red, I can hold them!" Chloe called. "Grab the book!"

Red took in her surroundings. A few feet away, suspended in midair, was a huge chandelier. If she could make the jump, maybe she could reach the bookshelf. But if she fell . . .

She had to try. Red leapt from the balcony and grabbed hold of the side of the chandelier, using all her momentum to swing to where they'd seen the cookbook. She reached out, and her fingers made contact—but she was still too far. The book slipped from her grasp and fell to the floor below her.

Red jumped down onto the round table. Commanded by the stone owl, the swords turned their attention to Red—but Chloe, thinking fast, grabbed a decorative shield off the wall and tossed it to her in a spinning arc.

Chloe took shelter under the table while Red spotted the owl and called out, "Hey! Birdbrain!"

She flung the shield at the owl, and the bird hit the ground with a thud. As soon as it did, the swords began to disintegrate in midair.

"Did you see that?" asked Chloe.

"No bird, no swords," said Red.

Slowly, Red crept along the floor, closer to the fallen owl. It had landed directly next to *The Sorcerer's Cookbook*. She had to try to grab the book.

But above the table, where neither girl could see, a swirl of mist had appeared. It twisted and spun, becoming more and more solid until . . .

A massive suit of armor wielding its own sword stood in its place. It leapt down from the table and prepared to attack Red—and with the knight providing a distraction, the owl took flight with the cookbook in its talons.

Red slid back on the ground, retreating from the knight's swinging sword.

As the owl approached the fireplace with the book, Chloe panicked. She looked around, searching for anything that could help her stop it. And then she saw them: her glass boots.

She pulled them off quickly, and with one last look at the gift her mother had given her, she hurled them at the owl. The glass shattered loudly when it hit the owl, forcing it to drop the book.

Instantly, the knight began to dissipate into thin air. Red jumped up and ran to Chloe, then helped her tip the table on its side to block the fireplace so the owl couldn't escape.

Panting, Chloe looked at Red. "Are you okay?" she asked.

Red, still flooded with adrenaline, realized that Chloe had saved her life.

"Those were from your mom," Red said.

"It was time to lose the glass shoes," Chloe said.

Red nodded, impressed—but before she could say a word, she heard the office door creak open.

"Wow, what a *performance*," Uliana said, sauntering inside with the rest of the VKs. She grinned.

She spotted the cookbook on the floor. "I'll be taking *that*," Uliana continued as a tentacle shot out and grabbed it before Red could stop her.

"Hey, get your slimy suckers off that," cried Red. "I don't think so."

Red lunged toward Uliana, spoiling for a fight—but Chloe held Red back.

"It's over. There's too many of 'em," Chloe said. But there was something in her voice that made Red pause. With a nod, Chloe silently told Red to trust her.

And Red did.

Uliana studied the book greedily. Its cover was enclosed by a silver clasp, and it rippled with magic. It looked just as it had in the vapors from Uliana's cauldron. Uliana unclipped the clasp, and the VKs peered over her shoulders to see.

"*Finally.* Let's see what kind of mischief you've got for me . . ." Uliana said, opening the book with hungry eyes, ready for dark knowledge.

Whoosh!

A cloud of green sparks shot out of the pages and hit Uliana and the VKs in the face. Instantly, they all froze in place. Their wide-eyed expressions were fixed in excitement, their smiles stretched taut.

The book blasted out of Uliana's hands and slid across the floor to the other side of the room. It snapped shut, and the silver claw clasp relocked around its cover. It was an enchanted booby trap!

Red walked around the VKs. She was stunned, but she loved watching them get a dose of their own medicine. Red waved her hand in front of Uliana. She could hear the VKs trying to speak, but their jaws might as well have been wired shut.

"Hex yeah!" Red said. She got right up in Hook's face.

Hook, straining to break free from the enchantment, only managed to say, "*Rrrrrr*," before Red tipped him over and he fell, stiff as a board.

Red grinned and yanked Hook's pirate boots off his immobilized legs.

She turned to Chloe. "New shoes? My treat."

"Thanks," Chloe said with a smirk.

"How'd you know *that* was gonna happen?" Red asked Chloe.

The girls crossed the room to the book.

"Bridget said Merlin enchanted the cookbook so it doesn't fall into the wrong hands," Chloe explained.

Red stopped just as she was about to open up the book herself. She backed off warily. "Oh. Right. You should probably open this, then. These are definitely the wrong hands," she said.

But Chloe pushed it back toward Red. "No. You do it," she insisted.

Red squinted. "Umm . . . I'm evil like my mom, remember?"

"You're nothing like your mom, Red. You're your own person—you're a good person."

But Red shook her head. For some reason, hearing those words from Chloe meant something to her—but she couldn't believe them. "I lie. I cheat. I steal. I'm a lost cause."

"You also just stood up to a bully, and you risked your own life to save mine. And right now, you're saving Auradon!"

Red stared at the ground.

Chloe continued, "I used to think that being good was about following the rules. Turns out it's a lot more complicated." She locked eyes with Red, needing her friend to hear her out. "You do so much good, Red. I'm sorry it took me so long to see it."

Red let the words sink in. She really wanted to believe Chloe.

"You got this," Chloe insisted.

So Red took a deep breath, faced the cookbook . . . unclipped the clasp . . . and opened the cover . . .

The silver clasp faded away. Chloe gave Red a proud smile, acting like she had never doubted Red's goodness for a moment.

"Told you," she said smugly.

Outside the office, Morgie kept watch from his perch. All of a sudden, Principal Merlin rounded a corner, hurrying toward his office. He muttered to himself as he rushed.

"Blast it all! What is it this time? Peter Pan's shadow? *Or* the Lady of the Lake? Oh, if it is, I'll turn her into a tadpole right quick!"

Morgie's eyes widened and he let out a loud *"Awoooo!"* His wolf howl didn't seem to alert the other VKs that trouble was coming, so he tried again with a scrappy chihuahua bark. *"Ruf-ruf-ruf-ruf!"*

Merlin got closer and Morgie gave one last signal, a meow, like a cat's. Merlin paused, squinting into the darkness. Morgie fell silent, and after a moment, the principal resumed walking.

Back inside the office, Red stared at the cookbook in amazement.

"How'd you know?" she asked Chloe.

"Oh, I was like eighty percent, max," Chloe said.

"I could've gotten perma-frozen, and you were only eighty percent?"

Chloe shrugged. Then they heard footsteps and muttering at the closed door. It was Principal Merlin.

The door opened and the principal stepped inside, spotting the frozen group of VKs at once.

But Red and Chloe? They were nowhere to be found. At an open window by Principal Merlin's desk, the curtains swung in the wind.

Principal Merlin approached the VKs disapprovingly.

"Well, I hope you enjoy detention, since you've just signed up for *years*."

The VKs couldn't move, but a groan escaped Uliana's throat.

Chapter Fourteen

RED: It's time to go back to the future! Is that *giddiness* I feel? No, it's probably a delayed reaction to my first experience with sugar.

Red and Chloe burst into their dorm room, overflowing with excitement but trying to keep their voices down.

"Did you see Uliana's face when she opened the book? She was like . . ." Chloe imitated Uliana's look of shock.

Red laughed. "I wish I could see her while she's stuck at home the night of Castlecoming. I bet she's like . . ." She made an exaggerated pouty expression.

Chloe cracked up but then stopped abruptly. "Wait—are we *sure* that she won't be there?"

"Uh, yeah! The VKs are gonna be in detention *forever*. And even if they could go to Castlecoming, with no cookbook, there's no way they can do the prank. We did it!"

Red held the cookbook aloft triumphantly.

"We can go back!" Chloe squealed, her anticipation building. "We can go home!"

But something occurred to Red then, troubling her. "Yeah, but what if we go back and my mom is still . . . my mom?"

"Even if she is, you're not gonna end up like her," Chloe said, trying to reassure Red.

"And this"—Chloe indicated the cookbook in Red's hand—"this is proof."

Red nodded, appreciating the reminder that she was *good* enough not to be frozen because of being *bad*.

"You saved my mom's life." Chloe smiled, and Red finally smiled back.

In the early morning light, the girls made their way to the vine-covered balcony of Merlin Academy, moving as quietly as they could.

"I almost wish I could stay and watch my parents dance at Castlecoming," joked Chloe.

"Maybe next time. Let's get out of here."

They paused at the top of the stairs and faced each other. Chloe reached into her pocket and pulled out Maddox Hatter's golden pocketwatch. Instead of using it herself, she handed it to Red.

"Here. This belongs to you," she said.

"Ready?" Red asked.

"Ready," Chloe answered, laying her hand on top of Red's. She couldn't wait to get back to her mother—her free, safe, happy mother—and put this nightmare behind them.

Red pushed the button and the gold cogs erupted, encircling them. Blurry shapes and whirls of color swirled around them as the watch pulled the girls back to their own time line. Back to the present day. Back home.

In the same spot, but now many years in the future, flowers decorated every surface of the Auradon Prep courtyard. Red and Chloe looked down to see the commotion of the Welcome Day Ceremony below.

"There they are! Our moms!" Chloe said.

Anxious, they hurried down the stairs and pushed through the crowd. The ceremony was unfolding exactly like before. Uma was up onstage, addressing the gathered students and parents.

"I'm proud to be charting a new course into a bright future," Uma said again.

In the front row, the Queen of Hearts noisily shuffled her deck of cards, distracting Uma from her address.

"Do you mind?" Uma asked the Queen.

"I do, actually," the Queen replied.

To everyone's surprise, the Queen of Hearts stood, her rigid posture as impeccable as always. Red and Chloe exchanged panicked looks, and Red shouted from the back, "Mom, what are you doing?"

"Playing my favorite game . . ." the Queen said. She turned and revealed a new look the girls hadn't noticed from behind. She was still wearing red, but now her gown was playful and whimsical, not severe and harsh. Pink and white ruffles fell in soft waves all down her skirt. She did a waterfall shuffle with the cards. "Hearts!"

She threw the deck into the air, and the cards tumbled toward the ground. But this time, soldiers did not form—floating red heart bubbles did. Everyone oohed and aahed at the beautiful display. The Queen looked at Uma.

"I'm so sorry. I couldn't help myself! I'm just so excited for my daughter to be here," she said. She looked at Red with nothing but love in her eyes.

"Well, nothing I say is gonna top that, so . . . have a great year, y'all!" Uma said happily.

The students cheered as she stepped away from the podium. Heart bubbles still cascaded down on the crowd. Red turned to Chloe, who was marveling at the magic display.

"You did it. You saved our moms," Chloe said.

"You changed history!"

"No, *we* did it," Red said.

Chloe smiled, appreciating the acknowledgment.

The Queen approached Red at last and opened her arms wide. She wrapped Red in a big hug. Red held her mom tightly, finally getting the approval she had always wanted.

"You know, Mom, you actually are . . . really wonderful," Red said.

The party kicked off after that. A DJ set up a booth in the corner and dropped a beat, the music blasting from his speakers. Students and parents alike moved onto the dance floor, and Red danced with her mom—who had some moves! They had a blast, dancing and laughing. Chloe watched them connecting in a way Red never would've dreamed of two days earlier. Chloe smiled fondly, wanting to share that kind of moment with her own mom. She had missed her so much.

She scanned the pulsing crowd, looking for Cinderella.

And all of a sudden, there she was—turning

to find Chloe, looking so proud. For the first time, Chloe felt like she'd really earned that look from her mom. She couldn't believe it, but she'd learned so much by getting her hands dirty—and she'd learned so much from Red.

The courtyard was full of happy, excited students and parents. Red and Chloe had gotten exactly what they wanted.

But getting what you want can be dangerous—especially when you mess with the fabric of time . . .